*This book is dedicated to Konrad,
Spencer and Aurora. May they explore the
world in the spirit of Thomas Blue Eagle,
spreading friendship, understanding and joy.*

*Special thanks to Marcella Hague for her
advice, insight and encouragement.*

— G.M. and J.G.

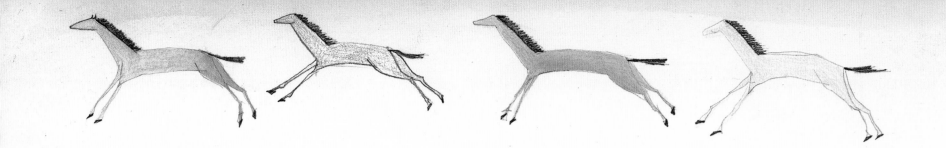

The Sketchbook of Thomas Blue Eagle

BY GAY MATTHAEI & JEWEL GRUTMAN

ILLUSTRATED BY ADAM CVIJANOVIC

chronicle books · san francisco

My story begins in 1885 when I was eighteen winters. I am Blue Eagle of the Lakota tribe and this is my sketchbook. It tells of my journey to the far away lands across the big water. First I will tell you the how of it and then I will tell you the why.

When I was a boy I lived in the Black Hills. After the wars with the white man, my people were moved to Pine Ridge Reservation. It was a dry place with a clump of wooden houses, old worn tipis and a nearby mission being built by men in black robes. The next winter my father sent me away to Carlisle, Pennsylvania to learn white man's skills. After six long years at the Carlisle School, I could hardly wait to go home. But when I returned, I found no honor, no work and no joy—only great hunger and sorrow.

White soldiers had wiped away the footprints of the Lakota from our lands. I did not want to disappear as well, penned up on such a small spot of earth. So I went away to a hidden place to think in silence, to see with my heart. I asked the Great Powers for help. Just as night was growing old I had a dream.

A line of wild horses raced through the tall grasses. They were led by a pale grey stallion with a blanket of stars on his back. I heard the voice of my grandfather say, "Ride the pale stallion. He will carry you to knowledge that will make our people proud once again." The stallion whinnied and beckoned with his head. The herd circled and streaked away. A great plume of dust swirled up and filled my eyes. I awoke.

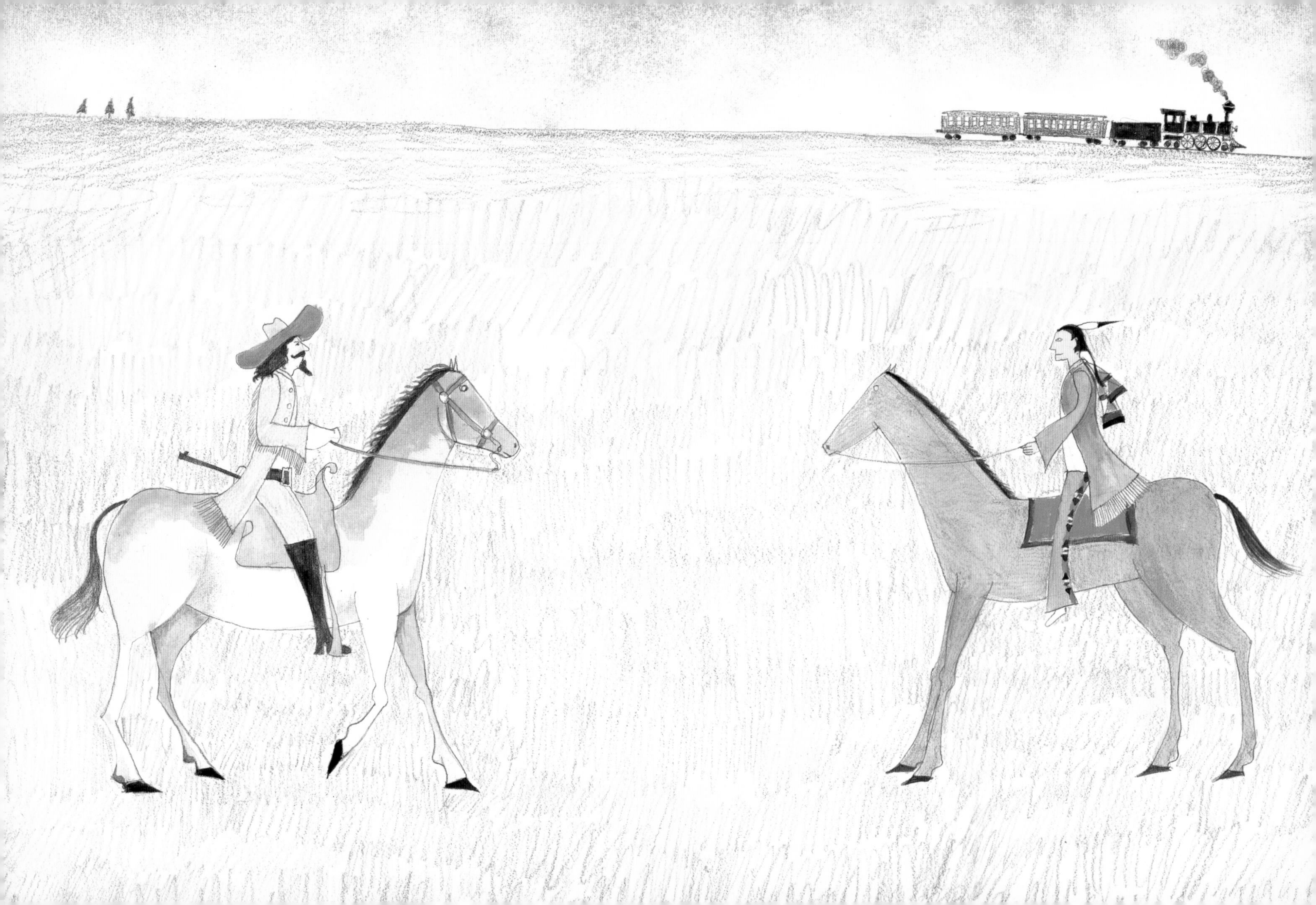

I rode back to Pine Ridge. A letter was waiting for me with the United States Indian Agent. It was from Buffalo Bill Cody, a white buffalo hunter with long brown hair. He was coming to the agency because he wanted me to help him with a show he was planning. He knew I was an English talker and had riding skills. When Cody arrived he told me about a long journey I could take to show the whites everywhere how a Lakota man could ride and shoot. Cody was sure city people would pay money to see a show with him and his horseback Indians. He promised to pay me well. He asked me to gather other Lakota men to join him. He promised to give us the pick of his herd. He promised me his famous buffalo runner. Cody wanted us to act out the very same life the white people had ended by killing the buffalo. We both wanted that life back again.

I thought hard about Cody's offer. Horses are Lakota wealth. Money is white man's wealth. If I joined Cody's show I could have both. I could have a ranch, a family and take good care of my father. I agreed to round up riders for the show. This was the how and the why for my long journey to white man's cities and the world across the big water.

I told Cody to hold a contest at Pine Ridge to see who were the best riders and to offer the winners money. That might persuade some of the Lakota men to join his traveling show. The Indian Agent said Cody could have his contest. Dark Moon, one of the Lakota men, had a string of horses in a little canyon nearby. He had captured them from the wild and tamed them. But he did not share them. Cody needed these horses for the race. He had to pay Dark Moon to use them.

Dark Moon had enough horses to buy a wife. He wanted to marry a girl named Echo. He had courted her, but she would not go under his blanket. Echo had promised herself to me. We had traveled the iron road together to the Carlisle School. There we spent hours filled with loss and loneliness. Then, we became friends and found the gift of love. We talked about running away from Pine Ridge, but where could we go? We had training and skills but most white people would not let us work for them. Without a job and money I could not take a wife.

Echo came to me before the contest. She asked me if I was going to go off with Cody. I told her my heart did not want to leave her, but if I made enough money to buy a herd of horses and cows I could give presents to her parents and we could marry.

News of the contest spread across the reservation. Many riders made ready for the race. It was like the old days after a buffalo hunt. Everyone was excited and made bets. The riders lined up—Grey Wolf, Little Otter, Plenty Horses, Cloud Shield, myself and others. Dark Moon led out a great tall horse. He had kept the best one for himself. He boasted he would win. I did not agree. There were many better riders at the reservation. I was one of them.

Cody fired his gun and we were off, tapping our horses with our quirts. Cody had loaned me his own horse for the race. His name was Old Charlie and he was very fast. I took the lead. Soon Dark Moon's big horse caught up to us with long strides. He cut sharp in front of us. We bumped into each other and I almost fell off to the side. Plenty Horses overtook us too. I held on to my horse's mane and pulled myself back up, hooking my leg over his flank. Old Charlie was angry at Dark Moon. He bared his teeth, laid back his ears and ran even faster. One by one we passed the others. We charged by Cloud Shield and Plenty Horses. Then we galloped past Dark Moon and finished first.

Now the men saw that Cody was serious and willing to pay well for them to act like Lakota. Many agreed to join the show. Cody was pleased. A farewell feast was prepared to honor the men who were going to leave the reservation. We had roasted meats, tinned sweets and coffee from the trading post. It was a good time. We had jobs and now we could care for our families.

Plenty Horses would not come with Cody even though he had finished second. He had been to the Carlisle School with me and Echo. He had had enough of city living there. He did not want to perform for white men. He had a bitter heart. Dark Moon stayed behind, too. He had his string of horses which he kept for himself. He did not need more of Cody's money. He boasted he would even things up with me one day. I was his rival for Echo and had outrun him. He had a jealous heart.

When it was time to go, I told Echo that no matter how far I journeyed, she would hear the beating of my heart. My friends gave her all the things they had won from the betting—blankets, parfleches, pots, knives, belts, robes. They were gifts for her family. She gave me a pair of fine moccasins with beads of many colors—yellow for earth, rocks and hills; green for rivers, lakes and seas; blue for the clouds and sky; red for the great light of the sun. Echo said wherever I walked in her moccasins she would be walking with me.

Cody made us work hard all summer. In the Moon of the Popping Trees we were ready to open the show. Cody and his riders paraded down the streets of a very big city named for an Indian tribe called Omaha. Cody's riders were dark Mexican men in wide sombreros, white cowboys in chaps and high heeled boots, and Indians in war bonnets. When I had been in the East, the Carlisle people had thrown away our hides and feathers. Now these white people spent money to see us wear them. Cody was right. It seemed as if every man, woman and child in Omaha had come to our first show.

We rode splendid horses—roans, bays, buckskins, blacks and whites. The horse Cody gave me for show riding was an Appaloosa, the best buffalo runner of all the Plains. He was pale grey with a sprinkling of dark flakes on his rump just like the horse in my dream. I named him Storm. I gave him a buffalo and deerhoof necklace to wear around his neck. It rattled like hail beating on dry leaves when he pranced into town, sending a message across the land to Echo.

Our first act was a buffalo hunt. I chased the small herd that traveled with the show around in circles. In my mind I was back on our lands, flying over tall grass, shoulder to shoulder with other warriors. The show was a big success. From the start, I was its best attraction.

One day Cody brought his friend, a man named Remington, to meet me. Remington was a reporter who wrote stories and painted pictures of the West. He painted me riding Storm. He made a pencil drawing on paper and then mixed his colors with water on a dinner plate. He used thin brushes with fine animal hairs. Remington's picture startled me. It was like seeing my reflection in a lake.

Remington asked me to tell him about my people. I told him how the Lakota had come out of the earth and about our kinship with the buffalo, our horses and other animals. I told him how my grandfather had taught me to climb up the foreleg of my horse as a small child, how he made me ride until my horse understood me. How together we had learned to fly over the ground. Remington wrote my words down. His drawings and stories about Indians were going to be printed in white man's magazines.

I showed Remington the ledgerbook I had made at Carlisle School. My drawings were our way of telling a story. He asked me to make a Lakota drawing for him. I drew a warrior on a buffalo hunt. He praised my picture. Then he gave me this sketchbook and paint like his to mix with water. He showed me how to shade the colors inside my dark lines so my pictures would not look flat. He told me to keep a painted record of my travels. This record would be a way for me to share my journey with Echo.

To my fellow artist, Tomas
Best of luck
Frederic Remington

Remington followed us from town to town. He painted scenes of Indians with mountains and rivers and canyons. Remington had made good mind maps of our West.

One of Remington's reporter friends took a photograph of me with a white woman who had joined the show. Her name was Annie Oakley. Annie fooled you. She looked to be a tiny schoolgirl but she was peppery and full of spirit. She had a Smith & Wesson revolver and an L.C. Smith shotgun. She was the best shot in America. Annie could shoot an apple from the head of a dog and slice a playing card in two. Sitting Bull, one of our chiefs who came to the show, praised Annie. He named her Watanya Ciscila, Little Sure Shot, and made her his adopted daughter. Annie and I became good friends.

Cody wanted an act for his two best shooters, me with my bow and arrow, and Annie with her gun. Cody said it would make the show more exciting. We practiced so we did not miss. We stood at opposite ends of the field. I shot. At the high point of the arrow's arc Annie shot. Her bullet split my arrow in two. I quickly shot a second arrow and it hit a broken piece of the first. The crowd roared and Annie saluted me. Annie had grown up on the edge of our lands. She knew how hard our lives could be. She knew we had to hit our mark or we would starve.

After a few moons, Cody taught us a new act. Most white people expected to see Indians as wild killers in wild country, so he set up a painted backdrop of the Dakota lands. In this new act I led an attack on settlers in their log house. Each day Cody brought in hundreds of bags of leaves. He used a strange blowing machine and made a cyclone whirl in front of the painted set. Sudden storms and the deep winter snows were part of life on our lands. One time Cody's cyclone blew so hard it flattened the log house and almost killed us. A flying piece of wood hit me in the leg so that I could not ride for days. That night Cody came to my tent with cigars and a bottle of whiskey. He wanted to cheer me up. I took a drink of Cody's whiskey but it made my head spin like the cyclone.

While my leg healed, Cody had me wrap up in my buffalo robe and wear my eagle feathers. I sat in a patch of shade in front of the show grounds near the Indian tipis and riders' tents. City people came to take camera pictures of us. I sat so still some of the white people thought I was a wooden Indian. They were surprised when I could speak to them in English. I told them each feather I wore stood for a brave deed done to protect my tribe. This was called counting coup. We counted coup not by killing an enemy but by touching him in battle and capturing his spirit. Each item of clothing and the paint on our bodies was a reminder of these deeds. The city people smiled and nodded. I was being admired for living my old life, a life that no longer existed.

Our show got so famous that Cody decided to take it across the big water to a place he called the Old World. The whites called America the New World, but this world was not new to us. Indians had lived here ever since the buffalo came out of the ground.

In America the crowds had clapped and stomped when I rode Storm. I wondered how I would be treated by Old World whites. They did not know about Indians. The Lakota believe that riding on the big water is dangerous, but if I did not go I could not make money to marry Echo. Before we left, Cody made me put the money I had earned in a bank. I asked the Great Powers to protect my money and me.

I had never seen water as big as the Atlantic. We traveled in a very large boat that bellowed like a buffalo and blew smoke. Indians and animals were all crowded into rooms with round windows. As we left the harbor, a swirling wind blew in a storm. The waves looked like mountains. All day long we slid from one side of the boat to the other. For many days I went without food because my stomach was so frightened it would not let me eat. The animals howled and cried. I went below to comfort Storm and sang for myself and the animals. On board that big boat, I was seasick, homesick and heartsick.

My first look at England was of high white cliffs rising out of the waters like those on the banks of the Missouri River. When my feet finally touched land I rubbed my face with earth and thanked the Great Powers for bringing me there safely. I put on the moccasins Echo had given me.

We traveled with our animals on an iron road. I thought there would be forests like we had in our land. Instead, all I saw were big cities with many buildings. That first night we camped in the Olympia Theatre in London, the largest English city. Our rooms were over a stage where we could practice. I put my buffalo robe on top of a bed of feathers and had my first good sleep in many days. When the sun rose an Englishman with a tall hat and gold on his jacket woke me up. I thought he was important and was sent to greet us. He spoke English but not the kind we had learned in America. We put on our capotes—hooded coats made out of white man's blankets—and went out for breakfast with Cody. The cook gave us cold toast and vegetables. Cody was angry. He told the cook that Indians were the stars of his show and we were to eat meat. He said we should never get leftover slops again. Then the cook made us a meal of roasted beef. It tasted wonderful after days of not eating on the boat.

When I returned to my room the Englishman with the tall hat had thrown my buffalo robe in a heap on the floor and was beating the feather bed. Every day he brought me hot water for shaving. He had no knowledge of Indians. We Lakota men have little hair on our faces. Most of our Lakota clothes could withstand the rain, but I could not wear Echo's moccasins in the muddy fields when we practiced outside. Each day my bare feet were streaked black. I saved the shaving water to wash off the mud.

In our lands I had hunted in the freezing winter and I broke the river ice to bathe. Yet I was never so cold as I was in England. It was always foggy and damp. Now I know why the English left their homes and sailed to America.

Cody had set up a race between me and an English champion. It took place in Surrey on a rare sunny day. The English rider was a tall thin man with a big strong mare. Bets were made. My Storm was half the size of the English mare. I had painted him with lightning marks for swiftness and power. Storm quickly outpaced the mare. The Surrey people were surprised. They wanted another race. This time they led out a stallion. Bets were doubled, but Storm won again. The English people insisted on a third race. One of their lords had a special horse which had beaten the best horses in Europe and was pure blood. Bets were doubled once again. The Indians wagered everything they had. A tiny man wearing a cap to keep the sun from his eyes mounted the race horse. I untied my braids and let my hair fall loose. I jumped up on Storm and we were off again. We pulled far ahead. Halfway to the end of the track I spun around and sat backwards facing Storm's tail. Storm won once more. The Indians grabbed up their bets and danced. The English were silent. They did not understand how a little Indian horse could outrun their big pure blood, especially after running two races. The English had never hunted buffalo. Buffalo runners are all sinew and heart. They race miles over the land to catch the herds. Storm was the swiftest of them all.

After the race, Cody whispered that it would be much better for show
business if I would mind my manners and let an Englishman win once in a while. In
London he sent us to polishing school to learn how to use spoons and forks. Cody wanted us
to act proper when we were guests of lords and ladies. I did not need all those fancy lessons.
We laughed about these English manners but practiced them to please Cody.

The English were surprised at the Indians' friendship with wild animals. We learn from them. They
show us their special powers and help us to survive. Eagle circles the sky and has keen vision. Fox is
persistent and gentle. Wolf shows strength through the pack. Badger never retreats. Bear has knowledge
of healing. Elk is agile and swift. The elk we brought with us from America was my friend. I called him
Hehaka, the Lakota word for male elk. I talked to him as I did to Storm. He understood. In the show, I
leaped on his back and rode him around the arena. No Englishman could do that. I rode on the hump of
a big bull buffalo, too. Our Lakota life had depended on the buffalo. They provided us with everything
we needed. We shared our lands with these sacred animals. They were our relatives.

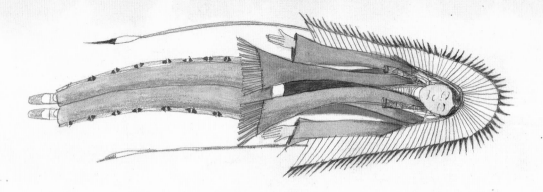

The English like it when someone is very brave and dies. For them the best act in the show was the battle at the Greasy Grass River, which the whites called the Little Big Horn. They thought Long Hair Custer and his men were heroes. The audiences hissed as we rode in with our faces painted black and dressed for battle. They did not know that Indians played the soldiers' roles too, because only Indians could make their horses lie down and play dead. After each show when we defeated the soldiers I counted coup.

The real battle was on a fine, fair day. Many Lakota bands, as well as some other tribes, had been camping by the river in the summer heat. They were not dressed for battle. Sitting Bull was there. He had dreamed that the Indians would win at Greasy Grass. The white soldiers had crept in from above the river to attack. They wanted to kill all the Indians or make them surrender and live on reservations. One of our chiefs called it a good day to die but the Indians did not die. Only the bluecoats died, the ones who had been foolish enough to attack a thousand Cheyenne and Lakota warriors.

Majesty came to see the show. Majesty was the queen of the English. She ruled over lands that stretched across big waters all the way to the sunset. We called Majesty, Grandmother England. She liked the show so much she saw it two times. Then she had the show moved to Windsor Castle for a jubilee feast and invited us to join her for tea and little breads. I wore Echo's fine beaded moccasins and my quilled shirt. I had heard of the power of Majesty and it pleased my heart that she welcomed me. I greeted her as if she were a great chief. I told her I had crossed the Atlantic just to see her. I was using English manners, saying things people wanted to hear. Cody called these white lies. I had never before spoken like this but I wanted to make Grandmother happy. She was sad because her husband had died.

Cody was glad that we had pleased Majesty. He gave each of us money for an English suit and an umbrella. We had worn scratchy wool uniforms at Carlisle School but the English woolens were soft and smooth. I picked out a fine grey cloth for my suit. We strutted down Bond Street in our new clothes. We no longer had the familiar smell of elk and deer. We had the smell of English sheep. We thought we were very grand but some of the townpeople pointed and laughed at us. They called us red wogs. I did not understand wog. Cody explained it meant someone with dark skin who was not a white man. It was an insult like our word wasichun, which means those other people.

In the Moon of Greening Grass we crossed over the water on a small ship to France. We took flat boats right to the center of Paris, sailing under many bridges. The city was in the shape of a star with big broad streets and old yellow buildings. Our boats docked by an island. Cody lived on a barge but we set up our Indian tipis in a great forest nearby.

The French did not speak English. Many of them did not know about our land in the west of America. They did not understand the meaning of what they saw in the show. They cheered for the Indians, not the soldiers. They laughed at the stagecoach attack. Cody was edgy. He was afraid the French did not like his show. Then Annie came out. The French admire young women. Annie did her shooting tricks with her special gunpowder. She had smuggled it into France in hot water bottles tucked under her skirt. The audience started to clap. We had to do our shooting contest so many times my bow arm got tired.

We became famous in Paris. The show was sold out. The president of France and the Queen of Spain came. Soon Annie's face and mine were all over Paris on poster boards. I sent Echo a photograph of me on Storm. I wanted her to know I was being honored in France as a famous Lakota warrior and was earning much money. I hoped she would wait for me to return.

We stayed in Paris for a long time. Remington came there to write about the success of the Wild West Show. He told me that Buffalo Bill Cody and his Indians were the most famous Americans in the world. He said he had to come to Europe to see real Indian life. In America, it could only be seen in picture books and paintings. Scientists too came to Paris to study Indians. They touched our faces and squeezed our arms. One day they tried to cut off pieces of my hair. The Lakota believe hair is sacred. I let out a war cry and jumped on a buffalo friend. The buffalo stuck out his long black tongue and chased after the haircutters. They did not come back.

During the day at the camp, I was often surrounded by people with easels and oil paints. They put my face on square bits of canvas. They called these portraits. Remington introduced me to some of his French painter friends. They were trying out new ways to add light to their paintings. I took out my sketchbook and water paints. Instead of making memory drawings in the Indian way, I did as they did. Remington wanted me to sell my sketches, but I would not. My sketches were for Echo, not to hang on French walls. I was walking on the white man's road, but I was not turning into a white man.

Near our camp there was a park called Zoo. The French people had caught strange animals and put them in little jails in a make-believe garden. Elephant was as big as six bull buffaloes. Giraffe was as tall as a lodgepole pine. Monkeys were like little dog men, jumping and chattering and swinging from their long tails. Tiger was a night hunter with powerful jaws. I ached for these four legged creatures. I saw the sorrow in their eyes. They missed their families and their homes. They had come from the Indies and from Africa. All day long they paced back and forth, hoping to return to their native lands. Their lives had changed like mine.

One evening Cody asked us to make a buffalo roast for his guests. We added venison, fried bread, cherry soup, turnips and wastunkala—dried corn we had brought with us. The guests came to our camp wearing silk and satin. They sat on the ground on blankets and hides and ate with sticks or with their fingers, Indian style. Their fine clothes became spotted with grease. They did not seem to care and they did not even give what was left to the hungry white children at the edge of the camp. No Lakota ever went hungry if there was meat. We always shared. The most respected man was the one who gave most generously. But the European chiefs did not understand giving. They kept their money for their palaces and fine clothes.

Sometimes when Cody enjoyed himself he acted crazy and began to shoot like a wild west outlaw. One night he shot out all the street lights with his Winchester rifle. People screamed. The police came. I grabbed him and dragged him back to my tipi before they could see him. They thought that Cody's wild Indians had fired the shots. The police did not speak Lakota or English and I could not say enough French words to explain anything. They took me away to jail—a huge stone castle filled with water and rats. I was shackled just as some Indians had been by American soldiers during our wars, although I had done nothing wrong. With my red skin I was an enemy, even in Europe. In the morning, Cody sent a Frenchman and some money. The police let me go back to the show. I wanted to leave and find Echo.

I told Cody of my plan to return. He was grateful to me for saving him from the police but he did not want to lose his star Indian. Cody told me he had a letter from the Pine Ridge Indian Agent. The United States government had never delivered the promised food supplies and my people were starving. I needed to keep on earning money for my family. Then Cody said that Echo had married Dark Moon. I felt such pain. Now there was no reason for me to hurry back to the reservation. I walked for a long way and cried inside myself.

My heart had fallen to the ground and I had no strength to pick it up. My artist friends tried to cure my sadness with songs and funny stories. They lived on the hill above Paris. Indians and the white performers liked it up there because it had music and dancing and can-cans. Can-cans were pretty girls who danced and yelled and painted their faces. These kicking girls were the best part of Paris. I did a dance for them using Lakota cries. One girl was so pleased she came over to my table and talked with me. I called her Kicking Legs. She called me Chevalier Rouge which means red horseback rider. I went back many times to see Kicking Legs and she came to see me in the show. One summer evening we danced the can-can together in front of the tall iron tipi the French were building up to the sky. We walked through the little Paris streets and down the big boulevards singing. But she was not Echo.

I decided to stay in Paris. I had painter friends and I was a big star. My belly was full of good food. In Paris my nose was as alert as a wolf tracking game, catching all the good smells—especially the pastries. I scouted out cafes where I could sit and eat sugar cakes, drink coffee and draw in my sketchbook.

The fame of the show spread to other countries and in the Moon When Plums Are Scarlet we went to Spain. We crossed over great mountains with snow tops and ended up on a barren plain. It was very cold, like winter in our hunting grounds. Some of the Indians got a strange sickness. Several had to be taken to the black robe hospital in Madrid. They were afraid of white medicine so I brought Yellow Horn, our medicine man, to visit them.

Yellow Horn prayed over our sick. He had painted his face black and blew smoke from powdered cedar needles, which he had taken from his medicine bundle. We sang at the curing ceremony. Our songs and music drew people to the ward. The black robe doctors rushed in. They herded the patients back to their rooms. But the little children in the hospital jumped up and down on their beds and called out for us. To make peace, Cody arranged for us to give a performance for the sick children. We did a buffalo dance and spoke about our lives on our lands. One of the Mexican men translated English into Spanish. I told stories about springs so hot that they cooked meat. I told them about red canyons so deep they seemed to have no bottom and how sound echoed through them for hours. Some thought these were tall tales, but they were true. Everything in our land was bigger and deeper and longer and farther than anything I'd seen in Europe. Thinking of those canyons reminded me of Echo and my heart ached once again.

In Barcelona Cody showed us a statue of Columbus who thought he had found the Indies when he bumped into America. That is why the English call us Indians. Many Spanish people followed him and brought horses. Horses helped us chase buffalo. Horses made our lives richer, but it was really a poor day for us when Columbus discovered America.

I saw a Spanish bullfight. Many men chased one lone bull. The leader lured the bull with a red silk cloth and then killed him with a long knife. The Spaniards did not eat the bull. They gave the ears to the leader as a prize. There was no honor in this hunt.

One day the owner of a famous fighting bull, Toro, challenged our buffalo called Tatanka. Toro pawed, then charged and knocked Tatanka down. Toro turned his back and snorted. Suddenly Tatanka rose up and struck the bull with his horns. He killed him. Toro was brave but he had turned his back on danger. I felt like that bull. I had turned my back on Dark Moon and he had stolen Echo.

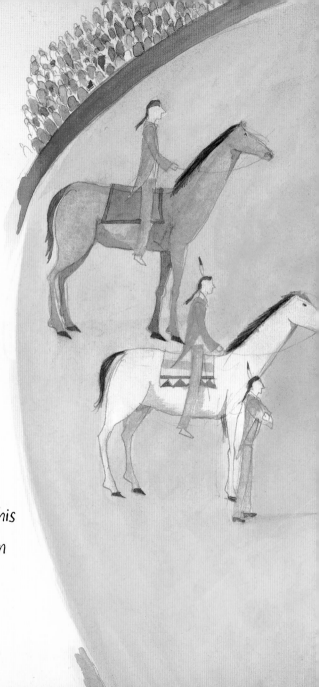

In the Moon When Wolves Run Together the Wild West Show sailed to Italy. The chief of the black robes invited us to visit him in Rome. The chief was called Pope and he had his own city, a painted palace and an army of soldiers. We met Pope at a large church covered with carved figures. The most important figure was Jesus, the son of the white man's Great Spirit they call God.

We wore our finest shirts and feathers to meet Pope. He wore a white robe and a tall pointed hat. At first I thought Pope's stick was a lance but Cody told us it was a shepherd's hook for catching loose sheep. Pope was a man of peace, not a warrior. Pope was pleased that I had read his Good Book at the black robe school. Pope blessed Cody who knelt and waved his hands making the cross sign. Pope wanted to bless us Indians too. He wanted us to pray with him to his Great Spirit and to Jesus. I did not do it at Carlisle. I would not do it in Rome. I know that there is only one Great Spirit but the Great Spirit speaks Lakota words to Lakota warriors. Those words cannot be the same as the Italian words the white man's God speaks to Italian shepherds.

After many weeks in Rome we made a trip to visit Venice. Venice looks like a dream. It is a stone city floating on a misty sea. The streets are water and called canals. They are attached to each other by little bridges. The white people think it is very beautiful but to me it was foolish to have a city in water. You cannot walk about but must ride in a canoe that is pushed along by men with poles. There are no trees. There is no grass on which to lay a blanket or set up a tipi, no place for horses or buffalo to run. No eagles soar above, only great flocks of noisy pigeons. The only good thing I saw in Venice was the light of the sunset on the dirty water. The colors made the water look like the rust papers inside the covers of this sketchbook.

One time when I was in one of the long gondola canoes, another one came up close. Venetian men showed us cloth called lace that looked like a spider's web and pretty glass beads. The beads reminded me of Echo and the moccasins she had given me. I decided to buy a piece of the spider's cloth. As I reached to pay, one of the boatmen grabbed my money pouch and pushed away. I jumped into the water and held onto his boat. He hit me hard and pushed me under with his pole. His boat tipped and I saw my shiny gold pieces sink down into the dark water and the spider cloth float away.

When we returned to Rome all of my dreams had crumbled like the ruins in the center of the city. My money was gone, my Echo was gone and I had no home. I had to start my life all over again.

One day Cody told us that an Italian prince had a famous stallion he said no one could ride. The prince offered a purse of gold coins to any cowboy who could stay on his horse's back for one minute. He did not want an Indian on his fine horse but none of the cowboys were willing to try. I quickly tied up my long hair and pulled down a hat. I wore a bandanna to hide my face. I became a cowboy.

I saw at once that the horse was full of fear. He pawed and rolled his eyes. I walked up to him and then turned my back and walked away. I did this many times. At first he shied but then he became curious and followed me. I placed my open palm beneath his nose so he could smell me. I gently stroked him and told him to listen to my heart. He understood my Lakota words. I swung myself onto his back. He did not buck. His head was high, his ears were forward. In a short time we rode calmly around the field. I counted coup. I had fooled the prince with his gold coins. Now I could get on with my new life.

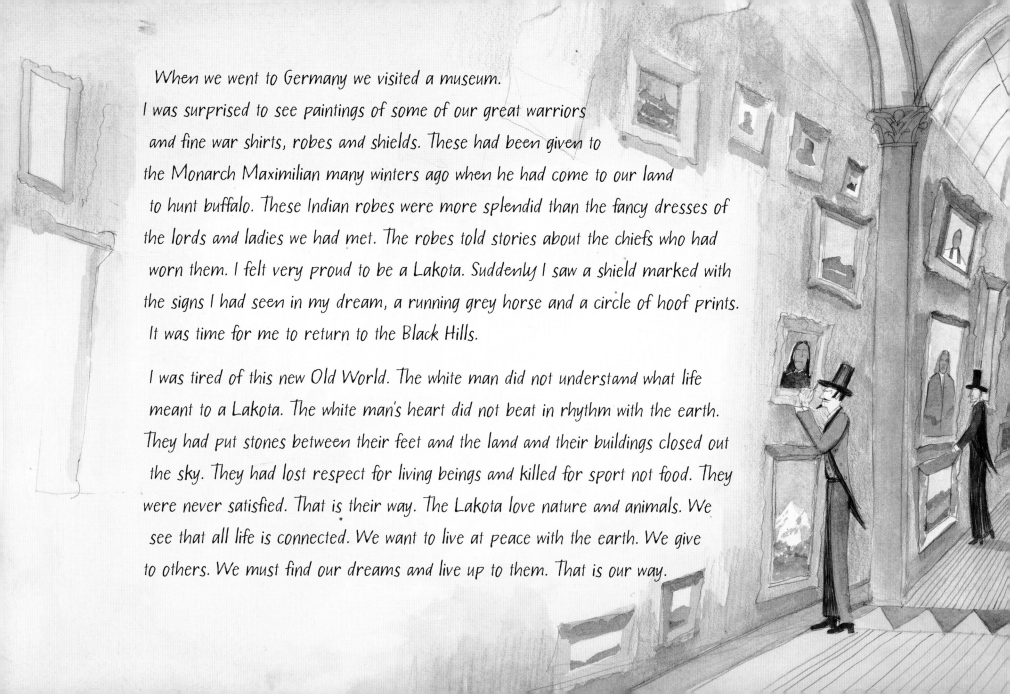

When we went to Germany we visited a museum. I was surprised to see paintings of some of our great warriors and fine war shirts, robes and shields. These had been given to the Monarch Maximilian many winters ago when he had come to our land to hunt buffalo. These Indian robes were more splendid than the fancy dresses of the lords and ladies we had met. The robes told stories about the chiefs who had worn them. I felt very proud to be a Lakota. Suddenly I saw a shield marked with the signs I had seen in my dream, a running grey horse and a circle of hoof prints. It was time for me to return to the Black Hills.

I was tired of this new Old World. The white man did not understand what life meant to a Lakota. The white man's heart did not beat in rhythm with the earth. They had put stones between their feet and the land and their buildings closed out the sky. They had lost respect for living beings and killed for sport not food. They were never satisfied. That is their way. The Lakota love nature and animals. We see that all life is connected. We want to live at peace with the earth. We give to others. We must find our dreams and live up to them. That is our way.

Cody could see I was homesick. He confessed that he had told me a lie about Echo and Dark Moon to keep me with the show. I was furious. That was no little white lie, it was a big black one. Then Cody gave me a gift to make up for tricking me. It was Storm. My heart was racing. I had Echo to go home to, the best horse in the world to ride and money in my pocket. I thanked the Great Spirit for so many blessings.

Storm and I rode to the edge of the big water and boarded another ship. This time as we crossed the Atlantic the sea was flat and smooth. When we landed in New York I went to the bank where I had put the money I earned in America. The money had grown much bigger. Then Storm and I took the iron road west. The trainman told me that Indians could not sit in the same cars with white people. To the trainman I was not a star, I was just a wild Indian with a speckled horse. In the box car I sat on the hay and studied my sketchbook. I wrote down the story of my journey. I thought about what I had learned in my travels. The most important thing was that there was no place anymore for Indian life in either the New World or the Old. I have to dream it into being to keep it alive in my heart.

After many days of travel I was home. There were many more log houses on the reservation but it was not a happy place. Most of the people were sick and hungry including my father. Dark Moon was not pleased to see me. He remembered the race I had won and now envied me my money and success. He did not want to learn about the world across the big water.

I was sad for my people. They had no buffalo to hunt, no way to count coup and earn respect. They were like blind men in a new place, reaching for dreams they might never catch. They were treated like children by the Indian Agent. They were cheated by the United States government. They were strangers in their own lands. When I showed them my sketchbook they passed it from hand to hand. Dark Moon snatched it. He said my book was full of lies.

It is true that the white man had tricked the Indians in their treaties with a black snake of language. Promises had slithered away, but my pictures of the white man's world spoke the truth. Dark Moon jumped on his horse and galloped off with my sketchbook. I chased after him on foot until I could run no further, but he got away. My gift for Echo was gone. My Echo was gone too. She had left to live in a white man's town a long time ago.

With a heavy heart I walked over to the little log house where my father lived. He was old and sick. I had to care for him. He told me that one good thing had happened. The United States government had allotted lands to the Indians while I was away. My allotment was next to his at Red Shirt Table, a grazing land with good water between the Badlands and the Black Hills. This would be a much better place to live than the reservation land. He told me the Lakota had always had to learn new ways, how to tame the horse, shoot guns and use money. He said, "Do not look back. The buffalo are gone. Buy your cattle and horse herds. Live at Red Shirt Table. This has always been your land. Care for it and it will care for you."

For the next two days I rode Storm over to see my allotted land. I was surprised. It was the same place where my dream had come to me and led me to travel across the big water. I had come full circle. I made a camp. When the sun came up I made a prayer to the Great Powers and thanked them for their protection. Again I heard the voice of my grandfather. This time he spoke of what I had learned. He told me that now I could see the world in two ways. First, I could see what was in front of my eyes, the green blades of grass, the hills dark with pines, the running streams. Then, I could close my eyes and see what was right at the edge of my vision, my hopes and dreams, my ranch and a Lakota family who would bring honor to our tribe.

Two winters later my father died. Our herds had grown and prospered. I had built us a comfortable log house. To the west I could see all the way to the Black Hills. In the east the morning sun rose over the Badlands, coloring the cliffs purple and red. It was a fine place to live but I was all alone.

One evening in the Moon When the Geese Shed Their Feathers, just as the shadows began to stretch across the plains, I saw a wagon approach. Someone was calling my name. It was Echo. She had brought all of her possessions and was coming to live with me as my wife. She had heard of my return. Echo was holding my sketchbook in her hand. She had found it at a trading post and she knew the book was mine. She bought it and came looking for me.

We sat on the porch together and turned the pages. I told Echo all about my adventures and how I thought I had lost her. She laughed and said I could never lose her so long as I wore her moccasins. Echo studied my drawings. They held the wisdom I had made real with paint and paper. That wisdom had shaped my dreams and now Echo and I would pass those dreams on to our children.

In Buffalo Bill's Wild West Show I rode across a
make-believe prairie with a canopy of canvas for sky.
My spirit reached out to thousands of people.

Time has wiped away my footprints from our lands
where the buffalo ran but I have left an Indian trail
all across the white man's world.

Afterword

The Sketchbook of Thomas Blue Eagle is the story of a fictional Lakota young man. As a child, Thomas had a life of freedom with his family and tribe on the Great Plains. But by 1878, the nomadic buffalo hunting ways of the Sioux ended and native people were confined to reservations. Thomas, like many other Sioux children, was sent to a boarding school in the eastern United States thousands of miles away from his family to learn the ways and language of the white man. While at school in Carlisle, Pennsylvania, Thomas and his classmates faced many new experiences and conflicts. He recorded these events in *The Ledgerbook of Thomas Blue Eagle*, an accounting book he filled with drawings done in the traditional pictographic style of the Lakota.

Upon his return home several years later, Thomas becomes disheartened. His people are totally dependent on annuities and rations guaranteed by treaties with the United States government, which were often ignored. Six small reservations had been created and 11 million acres of the former Great Sioux Reservation, covering the entire western half of South Dakota, were ceded to the public domain of the United States. One of these six reservations was the Oglala Sioux Pine Ridge Reservation near the Black Hills—Thomas's homeland.

Thomas finds his tribe struggling to adjust to the new life of trying to become ranchers and farmers. But the land is undergoing a drought. All are desperately poor. Many are suffering from disease and malnutrition. Many are heartbroken at having lost their former way of life. The old beliefs and customs are in danger of being lost forever. Thomas' people are concerned that their tribe will not survive.

The remaining reservation lands of the Sioux were even further diminished and divided by allotment to enrolled tribal members in accordance with the Allotment Act of 1887. The head of each family received 160 acres, and each person under the age of eighteen received 80 acres. Excess reservation lands were then opened to settlement by white homesteaders. These actions were taken by the United States government with the intent of turning the Sioux into self-sustaining farmers, a transition which would eventually lead to assimilation and the disappearance of Indian people as a separate culture altogether.

Foreseeing a dismal future, Thomas leaves the reservation and seeks answers and solace through prayer in the traditional manner of the Lakota vision quest. His answer: To discover knowledge that will enable him to make his people proud once again.

Because of his unusually fine riding and archery skills learned in his youth and his newly acquired skills in speaking, reading and writing English, Thomas is given a unique opportunity. He is hired as an interpreter and performer to travel to Europe with the Buffalo Bill Wild West Show along with other Lakota people. In the Wild West shows skilled riders, rifle and pistol sharpshooters, and Indians on horseback reenacted events from the history of the American West. Real Indians played the roles of historical warriors in mock battles with the cavalry and cowboys, much the same way they did later in Hollywood movies. The Wild West show performers became international stars acquiring fame and fortune like today's rock stars.

During his travels, Thomas creates a new book of drawings recording his many experiences. He continues the story begun in his ledgerbook in a sketchbook given to him by an artist friend. His pictographic art style changes as he is exposed to European artists. Through his drawings and his unique language expression, Thomas tells of his many adventures with such famous people as Buffalo Bill Cody, Annie Oakley and Frederick Remington. He tells of his encounters with Queen Victoria of England and Pope Leo XIII of Rome, both of whom did in fact meet with the Indians traveling with Wild West shows. Thomas' adventures in the great cities of Europe are based on actual accounts as recorded in the oral tradition by Lakota men such as my great-grandfather Stephen Standing Bear, Nicolas Black Elk, Rocky Bear and Red Shirt who traveled with Buffalo Bill Cody's show and similar shows from 1883 to 1917.

In time, Thomas Blue Eagle returns home to the Oglala Sioux Pine Ridge Reservation to take up a new way of life and to make peace with himself. His is a wonderful story of how one young Indian man finds strength and renewal as well as success through his Lakota identity.

Today, members of the Pine Ridge Oglala Sioux Tribe number only some 38,000 persons living both on and off the reservation. They still struggle to preserve their identities as Indian people. It is hoped that books such as this one will help non-Indian people come to appreciate and understand the Native Americans who are a vital part of this nation's legacy.

— *Arthur Amiotte,*
Lakota Advisor